WRATH OF THE LEGENDS

Adapted by Simcha Whitehill from the episodes
"Stopping the Rage of Legends!" Parts 1 and 2

No part of this work may be reproduced, stored in a retrieval system, or transmitted in any form or by any means, electronic, mechanical, photocopying, recording, or otherwise, without written permission of the publisher. For information regarding permission, write to Scholastic Inc., Attention: Permissions Department, 557 Broadway, New York, NY 10012.

ISBN 978-0-545-48378-0

12 11 10 9 8 7 6 5 4 3 2 1   13 14 15 16 17/0

Designed by Cheung Tai
Printed in the U.S.A.   40
First printing, January 2013

SCHOLASTIC INC.

ASH IS ON A QUEST TO ENTER THE UNOVA LEAGUE. NEXT STOP: DRIFTVEIL CITY.

I CAN'T WAIT TO CHALLENGE **CLAY**, THE GYM LEADER!

BUT CLAY ISN'T UP FOR THE CHALLENGE. . . .

WE'RE OUT OF REVIVAL HERBS. THIS IS **NO TIME** FOR A GYM BATTLE.

REVIVAL HERBS CAN HEAL SERIOUSLY INJURED POKÉMON. THEY ONLY GROW IN ONE PLACE — MILOS ISLAND.

HERE'S THE DEAL — BRING ME SOME REVIVAL HERBS AND I'LL BATTLE YOU!

YOU GOT IT!

THERE IT IS!

ASH AND HIS FRIENDS CILAN AND IRIS TAKE THE NEXT FERRY TO MILOS ISLAND.

MILOS ISLAND!

THE ISLAND OF LEGENDS!

WHILE OUR HEROES ROAM THE ISLAND, THEY FIND SOMEONE ELSE IN SEARCH OF REVIVAL HERBS. . . .

NICE TO MEET YOU!

HI, I'M LEWIS.

IT'S GETTING DARK, SO LEWIS INVITES ASH, IRIS, AND CILAN TO SPEND THE NIGHT IN HIS CABIN.

YOU'VE TRAVELED A LONG WAY. . . .

THIS IS THE ANCIENT *LEGEND OF MILOS ISLAND!* THESE DRAWINGS EXPLAIN WHY REVIVAL HERBS ARE ONLY FOUND ON THIS ISLAND.

IN ANCIENT TIMES, LANDORUS GOT CAUGHT IN THE MIDDLE OF A BATTLE BETWEEN THUNDURUS AND TORNADUS.

WHEN LANDORUS TRIED TO STOP THEIR FIGHTING, IT WAS WOUNDED. SO THE LOCAL PEOPLE GAVE LANDORUS SOME OF MILOS ISLAND'S SPECIAL MEDICINE — REVIVAL HERBS.

AFTER REGAINING ITS STRENGTH, LANDORUS DROVE THUNDURUS AND TORNADUS AWAY. TO THANK THE PEOPLE WHO HEALED IT, LANDORUS *TRANSFORMED* THE LAND INTO A *GREEN PARADISE.*

LEWIS' GOTHORITA RETURNS TO THE CABIN WITH A REVIVAL HERB. ASH LOOKS UP THE MANIPULATE POKÉMON IN HIS POKÉDEX.

GOTHORITA CAN USE ITS PSYCHIC POWERS TO CONTROL PEOPLE AND POKÉMON.

THAT HERB *DRIED UP* LIKE ALL THE REST.

GOTHORITAAAAA.

THE NEXT MORNING, LEWIS BRINGS ASH, IRIS, AND CILAN TO THE SHRINE OF LANDORUS TO ASK FOR HELP. THEY BRING STRAW TO LIGHT A FIRE FOR THE LEGENDARY POKÉMON.

THIS REALLY IS THE *ISLAND OF LEGENDS!*

LANDORUS, THE REVIVAL HERBS HAVE ALL **DRIED UP!** WE ASK FOR **RAIN** FOR MILOS ISLAND.

LEWIS ASKS GOTHORITA TO SEND HIS REQUEST. RAIN CLOUDS INSTANTLY GATHER OVER THE SHRINE!

GOTHORITA, GOTHORITA, GOTHORITAAAAAA!

WOW!

OUT OF THE CLOUDS COMES A LEGENDARY POKÉMON — BUT NOT THE ONE OUR HEROES WERE HOPING FOR.

TORNADUS!

WHEN ASH, IRIS, CILAN, AND LEWIS REACH TORNADUS' OBELISK, THEY CAN SEE IT'S BEEN DAMAGED! BUT WHAT — OR WHO — COULD HAVE CAUSED THIS DISASTER?

NOW THERE'S **NOTHING** TO STOP TORNADUS. . . .

GOTHORIIIIITA!

ASH, CILAN, IRIS, AND LEWIS RACE OVER TO THUNDURUS' OBELISK. IT TOO HAS BEEN SMASHED.

THOUGH MANY DECADES HAVE PASSED, THEIR RIVALRY IS AS POWERFUL AS EVER.

WHAP!

SWISH!

AN EPIC BATTLE HAS BEGUN — JUST LIKE THE ONE IN THE LEGEND OF MILOS ISLAND!

WE HAVE TO STOP THEM!

BUT NOT EVERYONE IS UNHAPPY ABOUT THE TROUBLE THEY'VE MADE DOUBLE. . . .

WE **DESTROYED** BOTH OBELISKS, AND TORNADUS AND THUNDURUS CAME TO MILOS ISLAND.

IT'S JUST LIKE DR. ZAGER SAID WOULD HAPPEN!

NOW WE JUST NEED THE **TWERPS** TO DO ONE MORE THING FOR US. . . .

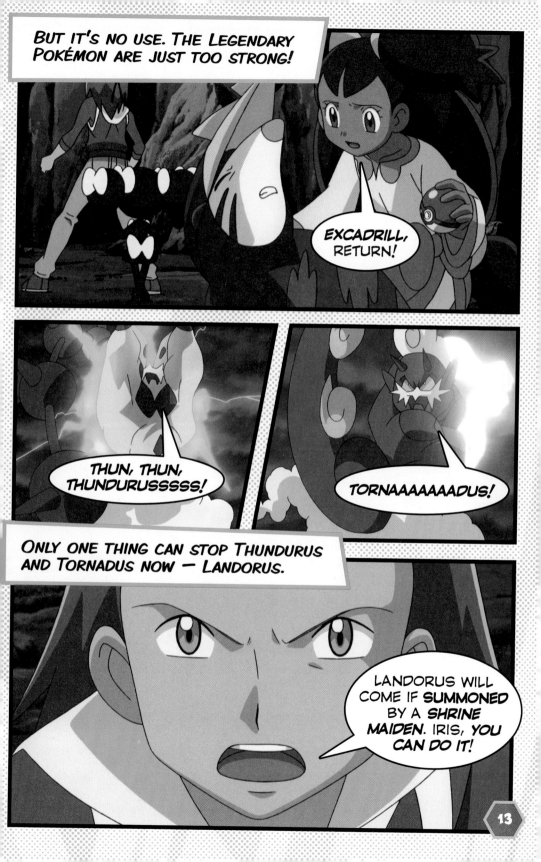

BUT IT'S NO USE. THE LEGENDARY POKÉMON ARE JUST TOO STRONG!

EXCADRILL, RETURN!

THUN, THUN, THUNDURUSSSSS!

TORNAAAAAAADUS!

ONLY ONE THING CAN STOP THUNDURUS AND TORNADUS NOW — LANDORUS.

LANDORUS WILL COME IF SUMMONED BY A SHRINE MAIDEN. IRIS, YOU CAN DO IT!

BACK AT THE CABIN, IRIS PUTS ON THE TRADITIONAL DRESS OF A SHRINE MAIDEN.

HOW DO I LOOK?

GREAT! LET'S HEAD BACK TO THE SHRINE.

WOW!

AT THE SHRINE OF LANDORUS, LEWIS PLACES FOUR MYSTERIOUS STONE BALLS AROUND GOTHORITA TO INCREASE ITS POWER.

LET'S BEGIN!

RIGHT!

15

THE ABUNDANCE POKÉMON FLOATS DOWN TO FIND OUT WHAT'S WRONG.

TORNADUS AND THUNDURUS HAVE DESCENDED UPON MILOS ISLAND! *LANDORUS*, I BEG YOU TO *STOP THEM!*

THUN, THUN?

TORN, TORN?

IF THE LEGEND IS TRUE, THIS SHOULD WORK!

EVERYTHING IS GOING ACCORDING TO TEAM ROCKET'S EVIL PLAN. . . .

DOCTOR, OUR PLAN HAS ENTERED *PHASE THREE.*

I'LL BE THERE IN A MOMENT!

MEANWHILE, LANDORUS ASKS TORNADUS AND THUNDURUS TO MAKE PEACE.

THUNDURRRRRRUS!

LAND, LANDORUS!

TORRRRRRNADUS!

BUT LANDORUS' PLEA JUST ANNOYS TORNADUS AND THUNDURUS. THEY TEAM UP AGAINST IT!

THUNDURUS FIRES FOCUS BLAST!

TORNADUS PACKS A PUNCH WITH HIDDEN POWER!

LANDORUUUUUUUS!

LANDORUS IS HURLED INTO THE MOUNTAINSIDE!

17

HERE, AXEW, REVIVAL HERBS!

AFTER JUST ONE SPOONFUL, GOTHORITA AND AXEW ARE INSTANTLY HEALED.

THANK GOODNESS!

YOU LOOK A LOT BETTER!

AX, AX, AXEW!

NOW THAT AXEW AND GOTHORITA ARE FEELING BETTER, ASH AND HIS FRIENDS WONDER HOW LANDORUS IS FARING. . . .

THEY'RE ALL BATTLING UP IN THE CLOUDS!

SUDDENLY, LANDORUS EMERGES BLASTING HYPER BEAM!

LAAAAAAAANDORUS!

BAM!

LANDORUS IS FIGHTING THE GOOD FIGHT . . . AND WINNING!

THUNDURUS AND TORNADUS ARE WEAK FROM BATTLE. LANDORUS TRIES TO REASON WITH THEM AGAIN.

LAND, LANDORUS?

THAT'S WHEN LASER BEAMS SHOOT DOWN FROM THE SKY!

CLAMP!

IT'S TEAM ROCKET! THEY'RE THE ONES BEHIND THIS EPIC BATTLE. AND OUR HEROES PLAYED RIGHT INTO THEIR HANDS BY ASKING LANDORUS FOR HELP.

TORNADUS! THUNDURUS! LANDORUS! NOW THEY BELONG TO US!

TEAM ROCKET! STOP THIS NOW!

GOTHORITA, USE SHADOW BALL!

GOOOOOOOTHORITA!

BUT THE POWERFUL ATTACKS DON'T EVEN MAKE A DENT IN THE LASER CAGES.

IT DIDN'T WORK?!

HUH?!

DR. ZAGER'S HELICOPTER COMES TO CARRY AWAY TEAM ROCKET AND THE THREE LEGENDARY POKÉMON.

23

FINDERS KEEPERS, LOSERS WEEPERS!

FORTUNATELY, QUICK-THINKING CILAN HAS A PLAN!

GOOD IDEA!

LET'S AIM FOR THE LASER SOURCE. ATTACK THE HELICOPTER!

PIKACHU, AXEW, AND PANSAGE AIM THEIR ATTACKS AT DR. ZAGER'S HELICOPTER.

AAAAAXEW!

PIIIIKAAAACHUUUUUU!

IT'S A DIRECT HIT!

UNABLE TO DODGE THE SURPRISE ATTACKS, LANDORUS IS HURLED BACK INTO THE MOUNTAINSIDE.

TORNADUS!

THUNDURUS!

LANDORUS IS IN TROUBLE!

IT'S INJURED! IT'S HOLDING ITS SHOULDER!

OH, NO. IF LANDORUS CAN'T FIGHT . . .

THERE'S ONLY ONE HOPE LEFT — LEWIS MUST GET A REVIVAL HERB TO LANDORUS.

GOTHORITA, SEND THE **REVIVAL HERB** TO LANDORUS!

THE REVIVAL HERB REACHED LANDORUS! SUDDENLY, THE ABUNDANCE POKÉMON RISES HIGH IN THE SKY, STRONGER THAN EVER! IT USES HYPER BEAM TO STUN THUNDURUS AND TORNADUS.

LANDORUS!

LANDOOOOOOORUSSSSSSSSSSS.

NOW THAT THUNDURUS AND TORNADUS ARE WEAK, LANDORUS CAN APPROACH THEM. PUTTING ITS HANDS ON THEIR CHESTS, LANDORUS SENDS THEM THOUGHTS OF PEACE.

TOOOOORNADUS.

THUUUUNDURUS.

AT LAST, THUNDURUS AND TORNADUS BURY THEIR BITTER RIVALRY.

WITH THE THREE LEGENDARY POKÉMON FINALLY UNITED, THE SUN SHINES DOWN ON MILOS ISLAND.

IT'S ALL UNFOLDED JUST AS IN THE LEGEND OF MILOS ISLAND. THERE'S JUST ONE LAST CHAPTER. . . .

PLEASE, **HEAL** THIS ISLAND. **RETURN** IT TO ITS BEAUTIFUL STATE, SO THE REVIVAL HERBS CAN **FLOURISH**!

FIRST, TORNADUS BRINGS THE RAIN AND THE WIND. NEXT, LANDORUS SPRINKLES SEEDS AND SUNSHINE. FINALLY, THUNDURUS SETS THE REVIVAL HERBS ABLAZE TO FERTILIZE THE SOIL.

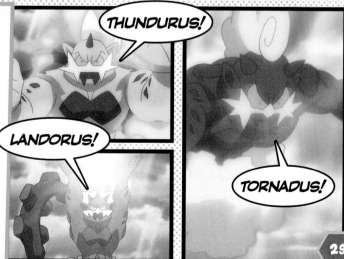

THUNDURUS!

LANDORUS!

TORNADUS!

IT'S **AMAZING** WHAT THEY CAN DO WHEN THEY WORK **TOGETHER!**

ONCE AGAIN, MILOS ISLAND IS RICH IN REVIVAL HERBS.

HERE COME MORE SPROUTS!

LOOK AT ALL OF THEM!

GOTHORITA!

ALL THE GRASS-TYPE POKÉMON ARE FEELING BETTER. LILLIGANT HURRIES OVER TO CELEBRATE WITH LEWIS.

LILLLLLLLIGANT!

LEWIS IS THRILLED TO SEE HIS ISLAND HOME BLOSSOM, JUST AS THE LEGEND PROMISED.

IT'S **AMAZING!** MILOS ISLAND IS BACK. TORNADUS, THUNDURUS, AND LANDORUS, **THANK YOU!**

THANK YOU!

LANDORUS!

NOW THAT HE HAS A POUCH FULL OF FRESH REVIVAL HERBS, ASH CAN'T WAIT TO RETURN TO THE DRIFTVEIL CITY GYM AND BATTLE CLAY! SO ASH, CILAN, AND IRIS HEAD TO THE FERRY TO CONTINUE THEIR JOURNEY. . . .

PLEASE TAKE GOOD CARE OF THOSE REVIVAL HERBS.

COUNT ON IT!

THANKS AND TAKE CARE, LEWIS!

GOOD LUCK WITH YOUR GYM BATTLE!

PERHAPS ONE DAY ASH'S TRAVELS WILL BRING HIM BACK TO MILOS ISLAND. . . .